The Colors of My [

Yellow sun, yellow clock.
Yellow means it's time to start my day!

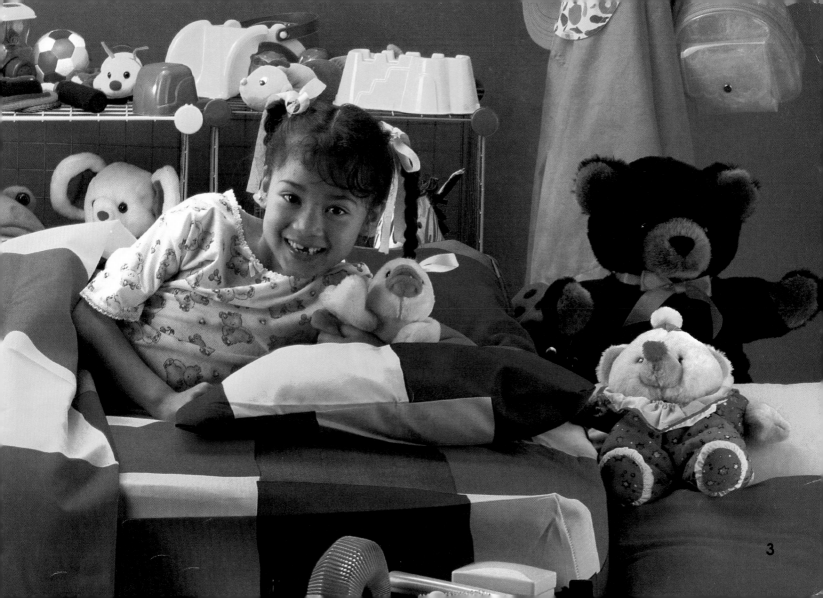

3

Blue bowl, blue cup.
Blue means it's time for breakfast.

4

Orange jacket, orange backpack.
Orange means it's time to go to school.

White paper, white chalk.
White means it's time to write.

Brown bag, brown bread.
Brown means it's time for lunch.

7

Green leaves, green ball.
Green means it's time to play.

Red brush, red paint.
Red means it's time for art.

Orange jacket, orange backpack.
Orange means it's time to go home.

Gray ears, gray paws.
Gray means it's time to play with my puppy.

Purple sky, purple plate.
Purple means it's time for dinner.

12

Pink soap, pink towel.
Pink means it's time for my bath.

Black sky, black bear.
Black means it's time for bed.